DOGS at WORK

Good Dogs. Real Jobs.

Written by
Margaret Cardillo

Illustrated by
Zachariah Ohora

BALZER + BRAY
An Imprint of HarperCollinsPublishers

There they go.

Off to who knows where.

What do they do all day?
And how could they leave us behind?

Don't they know. . .

. . . we have to play.

We have to eat.

We have to go on walks.

We have to cuddle . . .

. . . and eat again!

What could be more important than that?

What could they be doing that's so special?

And while they're gone . . .

who's going to keep us in line?

Or play dress up with us?

Who will help us put on
a beauty pageant?

Or listen to our favorite story?

What about the adventures
we want to go on?

Who will help when . . .
I mean, *if* we are
afraid of the dark?

After all, someone needs to keep us safe.

Someone needs to find us
during hide-and-seek.

Someone needs to bring us our mail.

Someone needs to take care of us!
Without them . . . who will know what to do
when we are sad? Or happy?

Or if we need help?

Who will tuck us in?
Who will give us kisses before bed?
Who will be our best friend?

What if they never come back?

They're here!

They're here!

I knew you would come back!

I was never worried.
Not for one single second.

But how about tomorrow
you take the day off?

To my husband, Luke,
my big yellow lab
—M.C.

For Waffles, who needs
to get a job
—Z.O.

BARKMATTER:
MEET THE REAL DOGS

Dogs have been with humans for thirty thousand years. That's a long time to live together! We've learned that dogs like to play, drool, sleep, and—especially—eat. But what a lot of people don't realize is that dogs also love to work. They may not carry a briefcase or wear a suit or a hard hat (though sometimes they do wear helmets), but dogs most definitely work. And believe it or not, every single one of the jobs in this book is real. Dogs are good workers because dogs are SMART. They can have a vocabulary of more than one thousand words. By comparison, most two-year-old kids know about three hundred words.

Some dogs are trained to do great work, and some dogs were just born that way. The important thing to remember is that all dogs need respect, kindness, and love, and then they can do the very best job there is—loving you back. Here are some of the very real jobs (and dogs) that inspired this book:

THERAPY DOG

Whether it's at the hospital comforting sick patients, on a plane comforting a nervous passenger, or listening to children read at school, nothing puts a person at ease quite like the love of a good dog. Even other animals, like horses, find comfort in having a dog nearby. Dogs can also help reduce stress. It has been proven that petting a dog or having a pet lowers your blood pressure.

LOBSTER-DIVING DOG

PB&J not cutting it for lunch? Drop that net and grab your dog! Dogs can be trained to dive into the ocean and catch lobsters in their mouths. Make sure it's a Florida lobster, though, because those don't have claws!

DOG GUIDES AND SERVICE DOGS

Dog guides are specially trained to help people with disabilities. They can provide assistance for blind people navigating busy streets and help people by opening and closing doors or turning lights on and off. Service dogs can detect if their owner has low blood sugar or sense a seizure before it happens. Some service dogs simply know when their owner is in trouble and fight to keep them safe, even learning how to dial 9-1-1.

TRUFFLE-SNIFFING DOG

Pigs used to help humans find truffles (delicious mushrooms that grow in the roots of trees) . . . until we found out dogs are better at hunting them down.

DOG SOLDIER

Thousands of dogs have served in the military. They sniff out bombs, search for wounded soldiers, and defend their handlers from enemies. Some of the bravest dogs in battle are awarded the PDSA Dickin Medal for their efforts. For an example, look into Chips, the dog from World War II.

MAYOR DOG

In 2014, Cormorant Township, Minnesota, had several candidates running for mayor. But it was Duke, a nine-year-old Great Pyrenees, who won in a landslide. His term as mayor was so successful, he was reelected in 2015. And again in 2016. And then once more in 2017. All in commanding victories!

HERDING DOG

Have you ever tried herding sheep? It's kind of like trying to catch one hundred marbles at the same time. It's hard for us humans, but for canines, like the Australian cattle dog, it's a piece of cake! Shepherds even have a special language used to communicate with their herding dogs . . . and even when they're not on the farm, herding dogs will corral the kids and adults in their family to keep everyone in one place.

SHOW DOG

Every year, the Westminster Kennel Club Dog Show recognizes the Best in Show, where dogs walk, run, and stand still during a careful inspection, all while looking very, very handsome. The show itself is the second oldest continuously run sporting event in America.

RESCUE DOG

Search and rescue dogs are some of the bravest dogs around, and various breeds are up for the challenge, whether on land or in water. They will often get a sniff of clothing from a missing person and then hunt down the scent. But they also know to search for signs of human life via the smell of skin, sweat, and breath.

FIRE SERVICE DOG

Though firefighters no longer use Dalmations to fight fires, these spotted

pups remain an important symbol for fire stations across the country. More than a century ago, before firefighters used trucks, they raced around in horse-drawn carriages. Dalmatians ran alongside them to keep the horses calm. Now, Dalmatians make loyal companions for firefighters. In fact, after the events of September 11, 2001, Ladder 20 in New York City was gifted a Dalmatian puppy named Twenty to boost the morale of the firefighters. Today, while some ladders still take Dalmatians to fire sites, they mostly take them to communities to help educate people about fire safety.

HAULING DOG

Dogs can haul mail, provisions, and people to remote areas where heavy snowfall makes access extremely difficult.

In 1925, two now-famous dogs, Balto and Togo, helped deliver an important medication called diphtheria antitoxin over six hundred miles through ice and blizzards to a remote town in Alaska, called Nome, saving the lives of the isolated citizens.

MOTHER DOG

Most mom dogs stay pregnant with their puppies for about two and half months. The size of the litter, or the number of puppies she gives birth to, can vary but is generally between five and six pups. Moms get busy right away nursing their puppies for about eight weeks. Then she turns the little rascals loose.

FURRIER FURTHER READING

BOOKS

Derr, Mark. *Dog's Best Friend: Annals of the Dog-Human Relationship.* Chicago: The University of Chicago Press, 2004.

Garber, Marjorie B. *Dog Love.* New York: Touchstone, 1996.

Masson, Jeffrey Moussaieff. *Dogs Never Lie about Love: Reflections on the Emotional World of Dogs.* New York: Three Rivers Press, 1998.

Méry, Fernand. *The Life, History, and Magic of the Dog.* New York: Madison Square Press, 1970.

Thomas, Elizabeth Marshall. *The Hidden Life of Dogs.* Boston: Mariner Books, 1993.

ONLINE

Cooper, Anderson. "The Smartest Dog In the World." *60 Minutes,* commentary by Anderson Cooper, June 14, 2015. Retrieved from www.cbsnews.com/news/smart-dog-anderson-cooper-60-minutes.

Flanigan, Linda. "Making Comfort Dogs an Everyday Part of School." QEOD, February 26, 2018. Retrieved from www.kqed.org/mindshift/50580/making-comfort-dogs-an-everyday-part-of-school.

NOVA ScienceNOW. "How Smart Are Dogs?" pbs.org, commentary by Neil Degrasse Tyson, September 2, 2011. Retrieved from www.pbs.org/wgbh/nova/nature/how-smart-dogs.html.

Balzer + Bray is an imprint of HarperCollins Publishers. Dogs at Work. Text copyright © 2021 by Margaret Cardillo. Illustrations copyright © 2021 by Zachariah Ohora. All rights reserved. Manufactured in Italy. No part of this book may be used or reproduced in any manner whatsoever without written permission except in the case of brief quotations embodied in critical articles and reviews. For information address HarperCollins Children's Books, a division of HarperCollins Publishers, 195 Broadway, New York, NY 10007. www.harpercollinschildrens.com. Library of Congress Control Number: 2020938814. ISBN 978-0-06-290631-1. The artist used Acrylic paint on BFK RIVES printmaking paper to create the illustrations for this book. Typography by Dana Fritts. 21 22 23 24 25 RTLO 10 9 8 7 6 5 4 3 2 1 ❖ First Edition